BOXER BOOKS Ltd. and the distinctive Boxer Books logo
are trademarks of Union Square & Co., LLC.

Union Square & Co., LLC, is a subsidiary of Sterling Publishing Co., Inc.

Text © 2023 the Estate of Bernette Ford
Illustrations © 2023 Erin K. Robinson

This edition first published in North America in 2023 by Boxer Books Limited.

ISBN 978-1-914912-22-1

Library of Congress Control Number: 2023932433

For information about custom editions, special sales, and premium purchases, please
contact specialsales@unionsquareandco.com.

Printed in China

2 4 6 8 10 9 7 5 3 1

06/23

unionsquareandco.com

Interior and cover design by Jennifer Stephenson

The Magical Snowflake

Bernette Ford & Erin K. Robinson

BOXER BOOKS

It was late afternoon.
The children wanted to play outside.
It was cold–so cold the tips of their
noses turned red.

They pulled on their gloves and mittens.
Their toes inside their boots felt like little ice cubes.

It was the middle of winter but there was no snow!
The grass was brown.

The ground was frozen–it crunched under their feet.
They jumped up and down to warm their toes.

Ori looked up at the sky.
"I wish it would snow," she sighed.
And then, as if by magic, she thought she saw a snowflake
way up high. Yes! One very special snowflake.

Down,

down,

down

it fell

and landed

on her nose.

"Are you a Magical Snowflake?" Ori asked.
She shivered a little, feeling colder.
The snowflake

bounced
down
and
landed
on her
shoulder.

Ori thought she heard it whisper,
"Let's go. Follow me!"
She called out to the other children,
***"Come on,
follow me!"***

All of a sudden, it started to snow!
First there was only a little,
just a dusting of white on the frozen grass.
Ori followed the Magical Snowflake, walking fast.
The other children were right behind her.

"Where are we going?" Ori asked.
"Follow me," the Snowflake whispered.

Out of the park and onto the sidewalk,
Ori followed the Magical Snowflake.
Now the snow was falling faster.

The children skipped through the snow,
making fluffy clouds as they passed the houses,
making long tracks on the snowy sidewalk.

Mothers and fathers came outdoors, all bundled up,
admiring the colored lights around the doors and windows.
The snow was coming down faster and faster.

The snow was getting deeper and deeper.
The Magical Snowflake seemed to call the grown-ups
to follow the children.

Ori pranced down the street and into the town
listening to the Magical Snowflake.
The children followed, holding hands.
The grown-ups followed too.

Shopkeepers stood in their doorways,
watching the children dance down the street.
Workers had strung lights across all the streets in town.

The snow was so deep now no cars could pass.
The moon rose up in the deep blue sky.
The Magical Snowflake leapt off Ori's shoulder
and led her into the middle of the street.

The children followed, forming
a circle in the knee-deep snow.

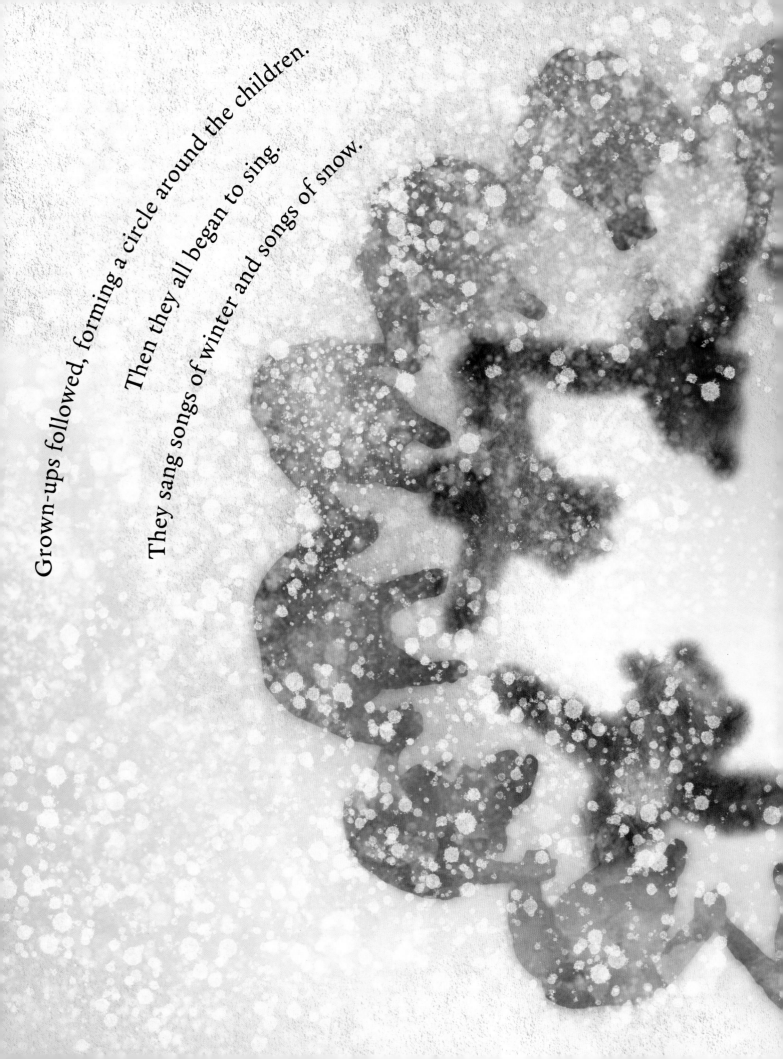

Grown-ups followed, forming a circle around the children.

Then they all began to sing.

They sang songs of winter and songs of snow.

They sang songs of joy!
They danced around the Magical Snowflake.

*"We
wish you
a merry winter.
We wish you a
merry winter.
We wish you a merry
winter and a town
white with snow!"*

As everyone sang, Ori watched the Magical Snowflake fly
up to the hanging strings of lights.
It swung from the string in the middle of Main Street.
It grew and grew, lit up like a giant diamond in the sky.

And there it stayed all through the starry night
and all through the winter.
Ori gave a happy sigh.
Winter was really here at last.